A secret message . . .

I grabbed a float and ran out into the water. I climbed on and paddled my arms to move myself around. I wanted to get as far away from everyone as I could. The water was so shallow, I could see the bottom.

As I paddled away I saw a bottle floating in the water. I leaned over and scooped it up. It had a piece of paper inside—a message!

Maybe it was a letter from someone all the way across the world. Or maybe someone was stranded on a deserted island and wanted to get rescued. Or maybe pirates had captured someone, and they were trying to get help. I could be a hero!

Bantam Books in the SWEET VALLEY KIDS series

JESSICA'S SECRET FRIEND

Written by
Molly Mia Stewart

Created by
FRANCINE PASCAL

Illustrated by
Marcy Ramsey

BANTAM BOOKS
NEW YORK · TORONTO · LONDON · SYDNEY · AUCKLAND

RL 2, 005-008

JESSICA'S SECRET FRIEND
A Bantam Book / July 1997

Sweet Valley High® and *Sweet Valley Kids®* *are*
registered trademarks of Francine Pascal.

Conceived by Francine Pascal.

Produced by Daniel Weiss Associates, Inc.
33 West 17th Street
New York, NY 10011.

Cover art by Wayne Alfano.

ISBN: 0-553-48338-2

Published simultaneously in the United States and Canada

Bantam Books are published by Bantam Books, a division of Bantam
Doubleday Dell Publishing Group, Inc. Its trademark, consisting of the
words "Bantam Books" and the portrayal of a rooster, is Registered in the
U.S. Patent and Trademark Office and in other countries. Marca
Registrada. Bantam Books, 1540 Broadway, New York, New York 10036.

PRINTED IN THE UNITED STATES OF AMERICA

OPM   0 9 8 7 6 5 4 3 2 1

To Katelyn Ryan

CHAPTER 1

The Big Fight

"Let's play dress up, Jessica," my best friend, Lila Fowler, said. She was digging through my closet. "I want to wear that pretty yellow dress of yours."

"Mom won't let me play in that," I said. "Let's look in the dress up box instead." I dragged out the box from under my bed and opened the lid. "We can wear these old ballerina costumes."

Lila shook her head no. "We wore those last time."

"How about these?" I held up two long skirts. "We could pretend to be pioneer women."

"That's boring." Lila went back to the closet. "I know! I can wear Elizabeth's pink ruffly dress, and you can wear yours. We'll be twins."

I chewed my bottom lip. I didn't like that idea. Elizabeth is my twin sister. I didn't want to be twins with anyone else.

In case you don't know me, I'm Jessica Wakefield. Lila and I are in second grade at Sweet Valley Elementary. So is my twin sister, Elizabeth, of course.

Elizabeth and I look alike, but we don't act alike. Elizabeth likes to do schoolwork, but I don't. My favorite part of school is recess.

Sometimes Elizabeth helps me do

my homework. I wish she'd do *all* of it for me, but our mother won't let her. Mom says that even though we look alike, we have to think for ourselves.

I *do* think for myself. I think I hate doing homework.

Being a twin is great most of the time, but sometimes we fight. That's because we're so different.

Elizabeth isn't the only person I get mad at sometimes. Lila drives me crazy too. Lila gets everything she wants, and she's always showing off. Sure, I'd like to get new clothes all the time too, but I'd never brag about it.

Well, maybe a *little*.

Lila started going through my closet again. She was throwing shoes and clothes everywhere. She pulled out my best black patent leather shoes. "These will look great with the dress." She slipped on a pair of my new lacy socks. Then she slid her feet into the shoes.

"Hey, goofballs." My pesky brother, Steven, poked his head in. "Looks like a tornado came through here."

I tried to ignore Steven, but he came in anyway.

"Here, Lila," Steven said. "Charlie Cashman told me to give this to you." He pulled a folded piece of paper from his pocket.

Lila wrinkled her nose as if she could get cooties just from touching it. Charlie's a mean, icky *boy*. But when Lila unfolded the paper, her eyes widened.

Uh-oh—it was the note Lila had given me at school! In the note Lila told me a big secret—that her mother wasn't going to take her to Fantasy Forest, the amusement park, like she'd promised.

Lila had been bragging about going to Fantasy Forest all week. She didn't want anyone else but me to know that she couldn't go anymore.

Lila glared at Steven. "How did Charlie get this?"

Steven shrugged. "He got it on the bus. So I guess you're not going to Fantasy Forest after all. Too bad."

Lila's eyes bulged. "You *read* my *note?*"

"Of course. Gotta go." Steven swung his arms around and around like propellers and he made a motor sound while he ran down the hall.

Lila's rosy cheeks turned pale. "Jessica, how could you give my note to Charlie!"

"I didn't give it to him!"

"You did so!"

"I did not," I replied. "I guess I dropped it. Or maybe Charlie stole it. You know how those dumb boys are. They're always trying to read our notes."

"I don't care! Best friends are supposed to keep secrets, no matter what." Tears streamed down Lila's cheeks.

"It was an accident." My face was getting hot. "I'm sorry. You don't have to get so mad."

"You're the worst best friend I've ever had, Jessica Wakefield!" Lila kicked off my shoes and socks and pulled on her own. Her shoes were on the wrong feet, but she didn't seem to notice.

"Wait, Lila, don't leave all mad—"

"I don't want to be friends with you anymore. Just leave me alone." Lila gave me a hateful look. Then she picked up my socks and threw them at me.

"Stop it!" I yelled. Before I knew it, I picked up one of my stuffed bunnies and threw it at her. Pretty soon we were throwing clothes and dolls back and forth at each other.

"Ouch!" Lila cried when my sneaker hit her knee. "I'm going home. And I'm not talking to you anymore. Not ever again!" She ran from the room and streaked down the stairs like a bolt of lightning.

I felt like crying. My stomach tied itself in knots. Then Elizabeth bounced into the room. Her mouth dropped open.

"What happened in here?" she asked, tiptoeing over all the clothes and toys.

I suddenly realized what a mess the room was. My side was usually sloppy, but Elizabeth kept her side neat. She liked her clothes folded and put away. Now they were everywhere.

"Ummm . . . Lila and I were playing dress up and—"

"You are such a slob, Jess."

"I am not!" I cried.

"You are too." Elizabeth made *oink* noises.

"Listen, Lizzie, I'll clean it up."

"You'd better. And you'd better not touch my things ever again!" Elizabeth stormed out the door.

I fought back tears. Elizabeth and Lila were my two best friends. Now my sister was mad at me. And Lila hated me.

I'd lost them both in the same day.

CHAPTER 2

No More Lila

"Everyone, since we're taking a field trip to the beach today, I brought in the fish tank," Mr. Crane, our new teacher, said in class the next morning. He was wearing a brightly colored shirt. It had seagulls all over it.

"What kind of fish are those?" Todd Wilkins asked.

"Tropical fish," Mr. Crane said. "Angelfish and butterfly fish."

Winston Egbert flapped his arms like butterfly wings.

Mr. Crane laughed. "I'm going to let you kids name them."

"How about Creampuff?" I suggested.

"You can't call a fish Creampuff," Charlie said. "That's too girly."

I looked over at Lila. Usually she would stand up for me. But today she just gave me a snooty look. Then I turned to Elizabeth. She stared at the fish tank like I wasn't even there. "We could call the yellow one Goldie," Lila said. Her nose was up in the air.

"I like that," Mr. Crane said. "After all, it is a golden butterfly fish. Goldie it is."

Lila smiled and twirled a strand

of hair around her finger. She didn't even look at me.

"I go to the beach all the time," Lila said. "My daddy has a *huge* boat. He takes me out in the ocean."

"You're so lucky," Sandy Ferris said.

"I know," Lila said. "Daddy lets me drive the boat sometimes too. Maybe next time we go boating, I can invite everyone along. Well, *almost* everyone." She glared at me.

My heart pounded. Would Lila really do something that mean? Didn't she want to make up with me?

I noticed Lila's notebook lying on her desk. On the first day of school we had written each other's names on the fronts of our notebooks.

Now Lila had taken a big black marker and crossed out my name.

Tears burned my eyes. I had to face it. No more Lila.

When we took our seats on the bus to the beach, Elizabeth sat with Amy Sutton and Eva Simpson. Lila sat with Ellen Riteman and Julie Porter. So I slumped down in a seat all by myself.

Elizabeth, Amy, and Eva talked and laughed. They looked like they were having fun. I wasn't.

"My daddy's getting a bigger boat," I heard Lila brag. "He's getting a whole *ship*."

Ellen squealed. Julie's eyes were wide. I rolled mine.

"Let's sing 'Row, Row, Row Your Boat,'" Winston said. His cowlick bobbed up and down as the bus went over a bump.

"We don't want to sing," Charlie grumbled.

"We'll sing it like seals." Winston cupped his hands around his mouth and made a silly face. Then he made a really awful sound. Winston probably thought he sounded like a seal. He sounded like a sick dog to me.

The other boys joined in. They made a loud mess of noises. No one was singing the same notes. And no one sounded anything like a seal.

I slumped lower in my seat. I could hear Elizabeth and her friends laughing. Lila was telling a story about deep-sea fishing with her father. Winston screeched out more seal music.

I covered my ears. It sure was lonely in the backseat all by myself. I should have been having fun.

After all, we were going on a field trip. But I felt miserable without Elizabeth and Lila.

"Everyone stay with the chaperones," Mr. Crane said when we reached the beach.

"It's beautiful!" Elizabeth cried after we'd all gotten off the bus.

Elizabeth was right. The deep blue water rippled and crashed against the shore. The clouds looked white and fluffy like big, fat cotton balls. Pretty rocks and shells covered the beach. I almost forgot how sad I was.

"First we'll hunt for shells and look for animal life," Mr. Crane announced.

Jerry McAllister groaned. "Don't we get to play?"

Mr. Crane grinned. "Yes. But

we're going to collect things first."
Mr. Crane pointed to a big box full of
pink, blue, yellow, and green buck-
ets. "Everybody take a bucket."

I tried to find a pink one, but
Sandy, Julie, Lila, and Caroline
Pearce grabbed them first. I wound
up with a blue one. A *boy* color. Yuck!

"Let's split into groups," Mr.
Crane said.

Elizabeth went with Eva, Amy,
and Todd. Lila joined Julie, Ellen,
and Sandy. They didn't even pay
attention to me. I began wondering
if I was invisible.

CHAPTER 3

The Message in the Bottle

My group was the worst group ever! I ended up with Lois Waller, Caroline, Winston, and Charlie. Caroline is always gossiping, Charlie is a big mean bully, Lois is kind of weird, and Winston . . . well, Winston is Winston.

"What's this?" he asked. He held up something that looked like a huge snake.

"That's a grapevine, Winston," Mr. Crane said. "Sometimes they wash up onshore."

"Cool." Winston draped it around his neck.

I shivered. It looked totally gross.

I found a few shells, mostly broken ones. But I thought a couple were really pretty. One was pink, and the other was tan with brown lines.

"Look, a little crab!" Winston yelled. He held up the crab in his hand. It was really small, but it still looked all slimy and buggy-eyed.

"Don't you dare put it on me!" I warned him.

"Put it in this bucket with water and sand," Lois said. "That way it won't die."

We watched the crab squirm in

the water and bury itself in the wet sand. I felt better when I couldn't see it anymore.

Mr. Crane blew a whistle. "Now we'll have some free time. If you go in the water, remember to stay in the shallow part. And everyone, stay close to the adult chaperones."

Elizabeth, Amy, and some of the boys ran over to play with the beach ball. Elizabeth was always playing sports with the boys, so I wasn't surprised that she didn't want to play with me.

I glanced over at Lila. I hoped she looked as lonely as I felt. I wanted to make up with her, even though she was being a snob. But she didn't look lonely. She was standing by Julie and Eva, who were making a sand castle.

"I'll be the princess," Lila said, dancing around like a ballerina.

"We'll be the fair maidens," Julie said.

Lila giggled. "We need a big castle so there'll be room for our servants."

The three of them wrote their names in the sand. It reminded me of how Lila crossed out my name on her notebook. I blinked to keep tears from falling.

I spotted Mr. Crane playing in the water with a few of the kids. That looked like fun. And at least Mr. Crane wouldn't treat me like I was invisible. Since I already had my pretty blue flowered swimsuit on under my sundress, it was easy to get changed.

I grabbed a float and ran out into the water. I climbed on and paddled my arms to move myself around. I wanted to get as far away from everyone as I could. The water was so shallow, I could see the bottom.

As I paddled away I saw a bottle floating in the water. I leaned over and scooped it up. It had a piece of paper inside—a message!

Maybe it was a letter from someone all the way across the world. Or maybe someone was stranded on a deserted island and wanted to get rescued. Or maybe pirates had captured someone, and they were trying to get help. I could be a hero!

I hid the bottle in the crook of my arm and tried to pull out the paper. But Winston dove in the water.

"I'm a shark," he hollered. He made big splashes that bounced my float around.

Jerry and Charlie flopped into the water and lunged up beside me. I held the bottle tight while they made waves. Then Jerry dropped a little baby crab on my float!

"Eeek!" I screamed. The crab wiggled around on my float. I thought it might poke a hole in it with its pinchy claws. Then I thought it might poke *me* with its pinchy claws. "That's not funny, Jerry! Get it off now!"

"I'll get it." Winston dove for it and slapped my float so hard, it flipped over. I tumbled into the water and kicked my feet and arms to stay afloat. My feet touched the bottom, and I managed to stand up. But the water soaked the back of my hair.

Thank goodness I still had the bottle in my hand. I hid it behind my back so no one would see.

Winston, Jerry, and Charlie laughed at me. Dumb boys! I rolled my eyes at them and settled back on the float.

When I glanced up, I noticed Lila standing at the edge of the water, laughing. Was she laughing at me too?

"Look, Winston's got monster hair," Todd said.

Winston had a big clump of seaweed stuck in his hair. It made me laugh. He raised his arms and acted like a sea monster.

The boys laughed and swam away, making monster noises.

Finally the boys were gone! I let

out a deep breath and relaxed. I glanced around to make sure no one was watching before I took the bottle from behind my back. When I shook it, the paper rolled out. It felt a little soggy, but I unfolded it anyway. One side had a note that was nice and neat, like it had been computer printed.

On the other side, in big red letters, it read: Wanted: A Best Friend.

CHAPTER 4

Wanted: A Best Friend

Hi! I'm seven years old, and I need a friend. It's lonely in my big house, and I don't have anyone to play with me. Not even my mom.

I like to play dress up and wear pretty barrettes. And I hate boys. They have cooties.

If you want to be my friend, write me a letter back. Put it in the bottle and leave it in the old hollow tree by the pond.

Your Secret Friend

My secret friend! I was so excited, I felt like jumping up and down. The girl sounded just like me. Except it was my sister, not my mom, who wouldn't play with me.

I read the note again. The girl liked to play dress up and wear pretty barrettes—me too! And she hated boys just like I did. We would get along great.

"Class, it's time to go," Mr. Crane announced. "Everyone get out of the water and gather your shells and things."

I paddled to the shore. Luckily my bucket of shells was right nearby, so I could hide my secret friend's bottle before anyone else could see it.

Charlie came up beside me. "You

were so funny, Jessica. Scared of a little bitty crab."

"Yeah, you're a scaredy-cat," Winston said. He meowed and made a scared face.

"Be quiet, you guys," I snapped.

Julie and Lila walked by me and laughed. Were they laughing at me again? Suddenly I had an idea. "You told Jerry to scare me, didn't you?" I asked Lila.

Lila's eyes widened. "I did not."

"I don't believe you," I said. "And I bet you told Winston to dunk me in the water."

"You believe whatever you want, Jessica. I'm not your friend anymore anyway." She stomped toward the bus.

"I don't need you," I muttered. "I've got a new friend now."

Lila didn't hear me. She just got on the bus. I didn't care. I couldn't wait to get home and write to my secret friend. The first thing I would tell her was that I needed a best friend too.

That night at dinner my mother asked, "Well, girls, how was the trip?"

I chewed my macaroni and cheese and thought about how mean Lila was. Then I remembered my secret friend and grinned. "It was great. I played in the water."

"It was fun," Elizabeth said. "I played kickball on the beach. My team won."

"I collected some pretty shells too," I said.

"And Mr. Crane asked me and Eva and Amy to do a special project for the class." Elizabeth smiled proudly.

I frowned. Elizabeth was going to be so busy with her other friends that we'd probably *never* make up. Well, it didn't really matter because I had a secret friend!

"Our class is going to camp out at the beach in a couple of days," Elizabeth continued. "We're going to sleep in tents and everything."

Mom smiled. "I heard about that. It sounds like fun. I bet you and Lila will stay up all night talking, Jessica."

I slurped my milk and kept quiet. I thought Elizabeth would tell Mom about me and Lila not being friends. But she just kept eating and staring off into space.

"I'm finished," I said, excusing myself. I couldn't wait to write to my secret friend. And I had a plan so I could write without Elizabeth seeing me. "Mom, can I use some of the extra sheets in the closet?"

"Sure," my mom answered. "As long as you put them away later."

"I'm going to the garage to work on my secret project," Elizabeth said.

"What is it?" Mom asked.

"I can't tell," Elizabeth said. "We're going to surprise everyone at the camp out."

I jumped up and ran upstairs. I was dying to know about Elizabeth's secret project, but I wasn't going to ask. It was probably something boring, like a paper.

I pulled two sheets from the closet and draped them across my bedpost to make a tent. One side

kept slipping, but I used rubber bands to keep it up. Elizabeth came in and got a box for her project. It seemed like too big a box for paper and pencils. What would she put inside?

As soon as she left, I crawled inside my tent with my pencil and a piece of paper and started writing.

Dear Secret Friend:
   I was really sad until I found your note in the bottle. I'm seven too, and I need a friend as bad as you do. I can keep secrets better than anybody. And I want a friend who won't get mad at me all the time.
   I like to play dress up and collect shells. Please write back soon.
                    Your Secret Friend

P.S. I don't like boys either. The teachers should give them cootie shots before they let them come in the room.

CHAPTER 5

Keeping Secrets

I rushed home from school the next day. I couldn't wait to go to the pond and deliver my note. I kept thinking about how my secret friend said she liked pretty barrettes. Since I had so many nice seashells, I could make her one.

After I got home, I grabbed some chocolate cookies and hurried to my room. I found the craft glue, my shells, and a wide plastic barrette and crawled inside my sheet tent. I picked out the smallest, prettiest

shells and glued them to the barrette.

It looked so beautiful, I wanted to
keep it for myself. But then I
remembered how sad and
lonely my secret friend
seemed. I had to give it to
her. I wrapped the bar-
rette in tissue paper and
rushed downstairs. I felt
like a spy about to go on a
mission.

"I'm going to the park," I told
Mom.

"Wait a minute," Mom said. "You
can't go by yourself."

"But Mom, I'm seven years old," I
argued. How could I keep my secret
friend a secret if I couldn't go alone?

"Elizabeth should go with you,"
Mom said.

I gritted my teeth. Spies didn't take their sisters with them on important missions. Especially when they were mad at each other.

"Elizabeth, will you go with your sister to the park?" Mom asked.

Elizabeth nodded. "I'll call Eva and Amy and see if they want to work on our secret project." Elizabeth called her friends, and we were off.

On the way to the park I carried my backpack with the barrette and the bottle hidden inside. Elizabeth carried her box as if she had a million dollars inside it. I wanted to ask about the project, but if I did, I knew she'd ask me what I had in my backpack.

I guess we both had our secrets now.

"I'm meeting Eva and Amy at the picnic table under the shade tree," Elizabeth said when we got to the park. "Don't spy on us, Jess. It's a surprise."

"I don't care about your dumb project," I said, faking a smile. "I've got stuff to do myself." Then I walked away and didn't look back.

When I saw the old hollow tree by the pond, my heart pounded in my ears. I took out the bottle and the barrette and slipped them both inside the hole in the trunk. Then I sat beside the pond and thought.

Where did my secret friend live? How often did she come to the park? Would she find my note and my gift today? How long would it be before she wrote me back?

I heard Elizabeth laughing with

Eva and Amy. I smelled wildflowers that smelled like Lila's expensive perfume. I swallowed the lump in my throat and stared at the tree. I hoped my secret friend found my note and wrote back right away.

I needed a friend more than anything.

CHAPTER 6
Mural Meanies

"Kids, today we're going to paint ocean murals," Mr. Crane announced the next morning when he walked into room 203. He was wearing a bright blue shirt with a green octopus tie. He put huge pieces of paper on two long project tables. Then he divided the class in half.

"Lila, you go with that group." Mr. Crane pointed to my table. Lila frowned and sat down in the empty chair with a huff.

I looked away. I really missed talking to Lila, even though she was acting so mean. Were we ever going to make up?

"Let's paint the ocean first," Charlie said. "Then we can glue shells and sand and plastic fish on it."

We used blue paint for the ocean and sky. We mixed in some white for the sky and some green for the ocean.

"We should use white for the clouds," Lila said.

Charlie crossed his eyes. "Real brainy, Lila."

Lila stuck out her tongue and painted a big white circle.

Ricky Capaldo used orange paint for the sun.

"I'm going to cut out some paper fish," Winston said.

"I'll help," Lois said. "We can use glitter for the eyes."

Lila kept painting clouds—big clouds, little clouds, tall clouds, and one cloud that looked like a shaggy dog.

Caroline glued sand on for the beach.

"I'll add the shells," I said, picking out my favorite ones.

"Look, I'm a fish," Winston said, gurgling. Blue paint dotted his face. He wiggled around like a fish and fell back against the table. When he stood up, he had a bright orange fish glued to his pants.

Caroline and I giggled. Lila giggled too, until she saw me. Then she chewed her lip and went back to painting clouds.

"I think that's enough clouds," Charlie said. "You can barely see the sky."

Lila painted one more. I knew she was trying to make Charlie mad.

"What about the plastic fish?" Kisho Murasaki wondered.

"Let's each choose one," Ricky suggested. "It should be our favorite color. Then we can glue them on and write our names next to them."

I looked in the box and saw a beautiful little pink fish. It was the only pink one there. I started to reach for it, but Lila snatched it first.

"Lila! You did that just to be

mean," I said. Lila knew pink was my favorite color.

"Who cares?" Lila glued the pink fish onto the mural and painted her name next to it in big letters. "We're not friends anymore."

"And I'm glad," I snapped. "I've got a *new* best friend."

"So do I. And she's a better friend than *you*."

"Well, my new friend is better than you too," I said. "At least she doesn't act snooty all the time."

"Mine doesn't tell my secrets," Lila replied loudly.

"And mine believes me when I tell the truth!"

"*Girls*." Mr. Crane frowned. "Please get back to work."

I stared at the ocean mural. It reminded me of how I found my secret friend's message in the water. I couldn't wait to go to the park after school to check the tree. If only I could meet my secret friend for real!

An idea popped into my head. Maybe next time I could! And if she lived close by, I would talk her into coming to Sweet Valley Elementary. Then I could show Lila I didn't need her anymore.

CHAPTER 7

Beach Babies

After school Elizabeth and I rushed to the park. Elizabeth ran to the field for soccer practice. I hurried to the tree. My heart thumped like a fast train. When I reached inside the hole, I didn't feel anything but rough tree bark.

My stomach fluttered. What if my secret friend took the bottle but didn't write me back? Maybe she didn't like my barrette. The idea made my face burn.

I decided to try one more time. I

stretched and pushed my arm down as far as I could reach. Then I felt something crinkly, like paper. I wrapped my fingers around it and pulled out a package. I reached in again and found the bottle.

My secret friend *had* written me—and she left me a gift too! I tore off the paper as fast as I could.

A doll fell in my lap. She had long, curly, dark brown hair and big brown eyes. And she was wearing a purple flowered bikini. A small plastic float came with her.

I took the message out of the bottle.

Dear Secret Friend:
I'm really happy you wrote me

back. Thanks for the beautiful shell barrette. I'm saving it to wear with my best dress.

I bought you this doll. I have one just like it. She's a beach baby. She floats in water. Write back soon!

Your New Best Friend

I hugged the doll to my chest. Then I tore out a piece of paper and scribbled another note:

Dear New Best Friend:

Thanks for the beach baby. I love her! I'm going to play with her all the time.

I really like having you for

a friend. I would like you no matter what happened, even if you goofed up. That's what best friends are for.

Maybe you could come over to my house and play. Write back soon and tell me if you want to meet me.

Your New Best Friend Too

I stuffed my note in the bottle and hid it in the tree. Then I played with the beach baby and her float on the pond until Elizabeth was finished with soccer.

"Hey, where'd you get that?" Elizabeth asked when she saw the doll.

"From a friend," I said. I could tell Elizabeth wanted to know who. But I didn't want to tell her until she told me about the secret school project first. Elizabeth tucked her soccer ball under her arm. For a second she looked like she might tell me her secret.

"I guess we'd better go," Elizabeth said, taking off.

"Guess so." I followed her. Elizabeth and I didn't say another word the whole way home.

CHAPTER 8

The Shell Necklace

When I got home, I ate chocolate chip cookies and dunked them in my milk. Elizabeth did the same, only she dribbled all over her T-shirt. It was funny how she didn't mind getting her clothes messed up, but she kept her room neat. I was just the opposite.

I went upstairs to find my shells. Since my secret friend liked the barrette so much, maybe she'd like a matching necklace. I could string the shells with holes in them and make Always Friends necklaces. She could wear the one that read *Always* and I could wear the one that read *Friends*. It was the perfect idea!

When I stepped into the room, my side was so messy that I realized I had to clean it up. Otherwise I'd never find my shells.

I folded my clothes and put them away. Then I stacked my books on the shelf. My seashells were underneath a pile of dress up clothes.

I found some heavy string in Mom's sewing box. I cut the string in two pieces. I made each piece long enough to tie around my neck and slip over my head.

Then I crawled in my sheet tent and sat on the floor. I picked out some of the smaller shells so the necklace wouldn't be too heavy. I even did a pattern. First I put the ones with the pink streaks, then the yellowish ones, then the brownish ones. Pink, yellow, brown; pink, yellow, brown. Then I painted the letters on the shells.

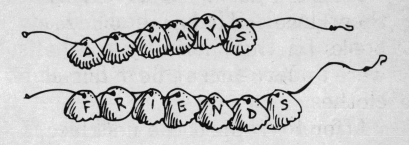

The necklaces were beautiful. I imagined my secret friend smiling when she saw the pretty shells. I took out a sheet of paper to write another note:

Dear Secret Best Friend:
  It's so much fun writing you.
I collected these shells at
the ocean to make you a
necklace. Your part of the
necklace says <u>Always.</u> My
part says <u>Friends.</u>
  If you want to meet me, I'll
be by this tree tomorrow
before dark. Wear your
necklace so I'll know who you
are. I'll wear mine.
              Your Secret Best Friend

After I wrapped the necklace, I
stuffed the note in my pocket
since I'd left the bottle in the tree
this afternoon. I wondered if the
girl had come yet. I ran down the
steps.

"Mom, can I go to the park

for just a few minutes?" I asked.

Mom glanced up from the table. "Only if someone goes with you."

I sighed, ran to the garage, and pounded on the door. "Lizzie, will you go with me to the park?"

"Don't come in here, Jess. I'm busy."

"Pllleeease?" I begged.

"I can't," Elizabeth said. "I need to finish this project before the camp out tomorrow night."

I leaned against the door and groaned. What was I going to do now?

Suddenly Steven barreled around the corner on his bike. Would he go with me? He'd bug me and tease me. And if I told him about the bottle, he'd laugh. But I didn't have any other choice.

"Hey, Steven, will you ride with me to the park?"

"What for, squirt?" Steven asked.

I chewed my lip. "I left something there this afternoon. I don't want Mom to find out."

Steven squinted. "Really?"

I could see the wheels turning in Steven's little brain. What had I gotten myself into?

"*Maybe* I'll go with you." He wiggled his eyebrows. "That is, if you promise to do my chores for a week."

Ugh! I should have known. Steven always tried to get out of his chores. He whirled his bike around and took off.

"Wait!" I shouted, running after Steven. He was my only chance. If I didn't get the note to my friend tonight, she wouldn't know to meet me tomorrow.

Steven peeled to a stop. "You'll do my chores for a whole week?"

"OK," I said. I didn't even cross my fingers. After I told Mom, I hopped on my bike. Steven raced ahead.

When we got to the pond, I told Steven to wait there. Then I hurried to the tree, reached inside, and took out the bottle. My secret friend had left me another message!

"What are you doing?" Steven yelled. He picked up some rocks and tossed them into the pond.

"Nothing," I said. "Just looking for my paper." I hid my secret friend's letter in my pocket and put my present and note in the tree. "I'm ready."

Steven jumped on his bike. "OK, let's go. I'm starved."

I raced home on my bike. Elizabeth was still in the garage, and Mom was baking an apple pie. It smelled delicious. I snuck upstairs to read my letter.

Dear Secret Best Friend:
I'm glad you liked the beach baby. Mine has long blond hair. I think blond hair is so pretty.
Please write me back and tell me where we can meet. I have lots of secrets to tell you.
Your Secret Best Friend

I folded the note and hugged it to my chest. What a great friend! I plopped on my bed and started dreaming about all the things we could do together. We could go to the beach. Play at the pond. Play dress up. Make cookies. Go to the movies. Paint our toenails and fingernails.

I was so happy! Not only did I have a terrific new best friend, but tomorrow night I would finally meet her!

CHAPTER 9

The Glow-in-the-Dark Camp Out

"OK, kids," Mr. Crane said when we got to the beach for the camp out. "Since you've already explored the beach, let's talk about the creatures in the sea."

"I wish we could see some seals," Eva said. "My mom said they nest around here."

"That's right," Mr. Crane said. "But they're too far out for us to see right now. So are the jellyfish and deep-sea fish that emit light."

"What does 'emit light' mean?" Ricky asked.

"It means 'to give off light,'" Mr. Crane explained.

"Like lightning bugs?" Elizabeth asked.

Mr. Crane nodded.

"Then those fish have their own built-in flashlight," Charlie said.

Mr. Crane smiled. "Sort of. Special ones do. It's called bioluminescence."

"Bio what?" Winston asked, scratching his head.

"Bi-oh-loo-muh-*neh*-sense," Mr. Crane said slowly.

I could barely keep my mind on what Mr. Crane was saying. Parent chaperones were all over the beach, watching us. I kept glancing toward the path to the park, waiting for a chance to slip away and meet my new friend.

"Scientists are using bioluminescence for medical tests now," Mr. Crane said.

"Huh?" Jerry asked.

Mr. Crane sounded like he was speaking an alien language. Of course Elizabeth was listening as if she understood every word he said.

"Bioluminescence is a kind of glow. It's a lot like your glow-in-the-dark stickers." Mr. Crane pointed to the glow-in-the-dark stickers he'd handed out. He wanted us to wear them so he could keep an eye on us. I wanted to take mine off so no one would see me sneak away.

"These stickers are cool," Ricky said, pointing to the glowing sand dollar on his T-shirt.

Winston stuck two stickers on his forehead. "Look! I have super-eyeballs!" he shouted. Everyone laughed.

"It's almost dark," Mr. Crane said. "If we wade in the shallow water, we might be able to see the sparkles of light."

We followed Mr. Crane and two of the chaperones. Mr. Crane hiked up his jeans and swished his feet around. Suddenly I saw sparkles that looked like glitter in the water.

"Look!" Elizabeth said. "It's really there!"

Everyone splashed their feet around saying, "Cool!" and "Awesome!" It was the neatest thing

I'd ever seen. I wanted to bring my secret friend back here and show it to her.

When I looked up, I saw Lila standing by herself. It was the first time I'd seen her alone since our fight. She pulled her jacket around her and walked along the shore with Mr. Crane. She looked kind of lonely, but I knew she was still mad at me.

"Time to roast marshmallows," Mr. Crane said. "Everyone gather around the campfire."

The parents had the snacks all ready. "Yum! They've got graham crackers and chocolate for s'mores," Lois said.

Some kids poked sticks through the marshmallows and roasted them over the fire. Winston crammed five marshmallows on his stick at the same time. The last one fell off and melted into the fire.

"You made the fire all goopy," Ken Matthews said.

Since everyone was so busy, it looked like the perfect time to sneak away. It wasn't quite dark yet, but it would be soon. If I didn't hurry, my secret friend might think I wasn't coming. And then I'd have no best friend at all.

CHAPTER 10

The Secret Friend

My heart pounded with excitement as I skipped down the path to the pond. The sun had already started to disappear, so I had to rush before it got dark. I felt as if I was going to a surprise party. Pretty soon I would meet my secret friend!

I slowed down when I saw the pond. Maybe I'd get a peek at the girl before she saw me. But what if I couldn't think of anything to say when I met her? What if she didn't like me? My stomach turned a somersault.

I smoothed down my shorts and combed through my hair with my fingers. The wind had blown it into a tangled mess. I wished I had put my hair in a ponytail like Elizabeth had.

I rounded the bend and looked at the tree. A squirrel scampered up it. Then I heard a noise.

It sounded like leaves and twigs rattling. I looked down and saw a girl with brown hair walking around the tree. All I could see was the back of her head. Her hair was long and straight. She had on a red jacket.

I held my breath. She reached inside the tree and put in the bottle. Wow! It was my secret friend. Then she turned around.

It was Lila!

I almost tripped over my sneakers. I heard my own breath whoosh out of my mouth.

Lila was my new best friend? The girl I'd been writing secret messages to? The girl who was lonely and sad?

"Jessica? What are you doing here?" Lila asked.

My tongue felt like it was stuck to my mouth with a whole jar of peanut butter.

"Did you follow me?" Lila narrowed her eyes.

I shook my head no. Then I showed her my Friends necklace. I'd kept it hidden under the collar of my T-shirt.

Lila's eyes widened in surprise. "You made this?" Lila pulled back her jacket to show off the Always necklace.

I nodded.

"I can't believe it!" we both said at the same time.

We started laughing and talking at once.

"I should have known," I said. "You like pretty barrettes and dolls."

"And you like to make jewelry and play dress up." Lila squealed. Then her smile disappeared. "How could you be lonely? You have Elizabeth."

Lila was an only child. "Lizzie and I are twins, and that's special. But there's nobody else like you, Lila."

Sure, Lila acted snooty sometimes, and she's always bragging about the things her parents buy for her. But maybe it's because Lila's lonely and is trying to hide it.

Now I understood why she'd been so mad when she thought I'd given her note to the boys. Missing her mom was the kind of deep-down secret you only shared with your very best friend.

"I didn't give the note to Charlie. Honest," I said, feeling teary eyed. "I'm sorry you didn't think I was a good friend."

Lila bit her lip. "I know you didn't give it to him. I was just embarrassed." Lila took the bottle from the tree and handed it to me. "I shouldn't have gotten so mad."

I pulled out the last message and read it.

Dear Best Friend:

I used to have a best friend. But I got mad at her, and now I miss her a lot.

I promise not to get mad at you. You're the best friend ever. I want us to always be friends.

Let's play together every day.
                    Your Best Friend

"I missed you too," I said. I folded up the letter and stuck it in my pocket. "And I'm going to keep this forever."

"We'll always be friends," Lila said.

"Best friends," I said.

"Better than ever." We laughed and hugged.

"We'd better get back before it gets dark," Lila said.

"Let's share a tent tonight," I suggested.

Lila grinned and nodded. "We'll whisper secrets all night."

We ran all the way back to the camp, laughing the whole way. When we reached the campfire, we saw Elizabeth, Amy, and Eva bringing out the secret box.

"We finished our project," Elizabeth announced.

"We made glow-in-the-dark wands," Eva said. Everyone gathered around when she opened the box and took out two sticks. They were painted glow-in-the-dark yellow and green. She waved them in the air. They really glowed! Everybody cheered.

"Here, Jess," Elizabeth said. "I made you a pink one."

I hugged Elizabeth. "This is so cool, Lizzie."

We all twirled our wands around and made designs in the air. Even Mr. Crane jumped around with his. Some of the girls tossed theirs into the air like batons. Winston tossed his in the air and tried to catch it, but it fell and hit him on the head.

"Let's lie down on our sleeping bags and write our names in the sky," Lila said.

"OK." I unfolded my bag and lay down beside Lila. Elizabeth lay down on the other side.

"Look at my name," Lila said. She drew the letters in the sky with her wand. It was pink, just like mine.

"I'm writing mine too," I said.

"I think I'll just write 'Lizzie,'" Elizabeth said. "My name has too many letters."

We all laughed. I felt so good, I thought I might burst. Elizabeth and I didn't have any more secrets. And Lila and I were better friends than ever.

"Look at all those stars," I said.

"I wonder how many there are?" Lila asked. She rubbed her neck-lace between her fingers.

"I don't know," I said. "But we'll

be best friends as long as there're stars in the sky."

"And that'll be forever." Lila leaned close. "You know what I heard?" she whispered.

"What?" I asked, giggling. I was so happy that Lila and I were telling secrets again.

"Mr. Crane said we're taking another field trip next week."

"Where?"

"I can't tell you." Lila smiled. "It's a secret!"

Where could Mr. Crane be taking the class next? Don't miss Sweet Valley Kids #72, **THE MACARONI MESS.**

Elizabeth's Crossword Puzzle

Elizabeth remembered ten things that happened in the story. But after she wrote them out, she erased a word or name from each sentence!

When you figure out what the missing word or name is, fill in the blanks. Then you can write the missing word in the matching crossword spaces!

Can you get all ten words right without peeking back at the story? Good luck!

Across:

1. Steven got Lila's note from _____.
2. Jessica wanted to call the fish_____.
3. Jessica used _____ to decorate the barrette and necklaces.
4. Lila painted _____ on the ocean mural.
5. Jessica and Lila's favorite color is _____.

Down:

1. Jerry scared Jessica when he put a _____ on her float.
2. The kids roasted marshmallows over a _____.
3. Winston and the boys tried to sing like _____ on the bus.
4. Lila got to name the fish _____.
5. Lila was upset that her mother wasn't taking her to _____ Forest.

Jessica's Word Search

Jessica wrote down ten of her favorite words from the story. Then she hid each one either horizontally (side-to-side) or vertically (up-and-down) in the word search puzzle at the bottom of the page.

Can you find all ten? Good luck!

ANGELFISH
BARRETTE
BEACH
BOTTLE
FRIEND

GLITTER
MARSHMALLOWS
SEAWEED
TREE
TROPICAL

```
B E A C T R O P I C A L
E F R I E N D W B I V H
A C Q U R O P I O E S A
C N I B A R R E T T E Y
H X T U O R F B T U A P
M A R S H M A L L O W S
H I E V W A U R E M E L
J T E F S P N R A T E K
B R U G L I T T E R D P
M I W Z I Y S P B M E A
I A N G E L F I S H R W
D I N S O R W Z H Q I A
```

Turn the page for answers, and another great activity!

Answers

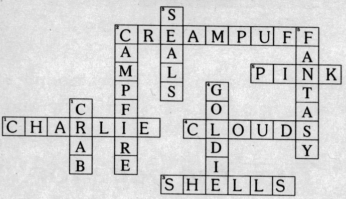

Crossword puzzle solution:
- CREAMPUFF (across, 2)
- PINK (across, 6)
- CHARLIE (across, 1)
- CLOUDS (across, 4)
- SHELLS (across, 3)
- SEALS (down, 3)
- CAMPFIRE (down, 2)
- FANTASY (down, 5)
- CRAB (down, 1)
- GODIE (down, 4)

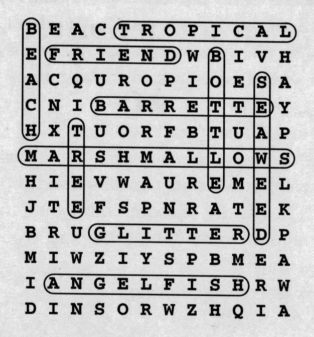

Word search solution with found words:
- TROPICAL
- FRIEND
- BARRETTE
- MARSHMALLOWS
- GLITTER
- ANGELFISH
- BEACH
- BEACH (vertical)

Elizabeth and Jessica's "Ocean in a Bottle"

Elizabeth and Jessica know about a special project that's easy to make and totally cool! The twins call it an "Ocean in a Bottle"—and now they're going to pass their secret on to you!

Make sure you have permission from an adult before you start. And don't forget to have an adult close by when you put your Ocean in a Bottle together!

Here's what you'll need:

1) a clear, empty plastic bottle with a resealable (twist-on) cap (like a soda bottle)

2) a bottle of baby oil (you'll need enough oil to fill half of the plastic bottle)

3) water

4) blue food coloring

Here's what you do:

1) Make sure the plastic bottle is clean and that the cap fits tightly. You don't want your bottle to leak when you're finished!

2) Fill the bottle halfway with water.

3) Fill the rest of the bottle (almost to the top) with baby oil. (Ask an adult to help you with this.)

4) Add a couple of drops of the blue food coloring to the mixture. The baby oil will stay clear—while the water will magically turn blue like the ocean!

5) Twist the cap back on very tightly.

6) Now turn the bottle on its side, tilt it back and forth, and watch the waves form and swirl in the blue water!

Now that you've made your first Ocean in a Bottle, you might want to add some special things to the water to make it look like a real ocean—or make it look really fun! Try adding:

☆ real sand (it will sink to the bottom)

☆ little plastic fish—they'll "swim" in the water when you tilt the bottle

☆ shells or pebbles

☆ glitter

You can even use different food-coloring colors . . . and turn the water pink, purple, or green!

At your next party, have a contest with your friends to see who can make the most realistic Ocean in a Bottle—or the prettiest!

SIGN UP FOR THE SWEET VALLEY HIGH® FAN CLUB!

Hey, girls! Get all the gossip on Sweet Valley High's® most popular teenagers when you join our fantastic Fan Club! As a member, you'll get all of this really cool stuff:

- Membership Card with your own personal Fan Club ID number
- A Sweet Valley High® Secret Treasure Box
- Sweet Valley High® Stationery
- Official Fan Club Pencil (for secret note writing!)
- Three Bookmarks
- A "Members Only" Door Hanger
- Two Skeins of J. & P. Coats® Embroidery Floss with flower barrette instruction leaflet
- Two editions of *The Oracle* newsletter
- Plus exclusive Sweet Valley High® product offers, special savings, contests, and much more!

Be the first to find out what Jessica & Elizabeth Wakefield are up to by joining the Sweet Valley High® Fan Club for the one-year membership fee of only $6.25 each for U.S. residents, $8.25 for Canadian residents (U.S. currency). Includes shipping & handling.

Send a check or money order (do not send cash) made payable to "Sweet Valley High® Fan Club" along with this form to:

SWEET VALLEY HIGH® FAN CLUB, BOX 3919-B, SCHAUMBURG, IL 60168-3919

NAME _____
(Please print clearly)

ADDRESS _____

CITY_____ STATE _____ ZIP_____
(Required)

AGE _____ BIRTHDAY_____ / _____ / _____

Offer good while supplies last. Allow 6-8 weeks after check clearance for delivery. Addresses without ZIP codes cannot be honored. Offer good in USA & Canada only. Void where prohibited by law.
©1993 by Francine Pascal   LCI-1383-193